Noisy Farm

Rod Campbell

PUFFIN BOOKS

It's daybreak on the farm.
'Cockadoodle-doo' says
the rooster.
'Wake up, wake up!'

'Woof, woof!'
Sam the farm dog is awake.
He can hear lots of
different noises.

Sam can hear a chugging noise.
What can that be?

It's the tractor
off to plough the fields.

Where's Sam?

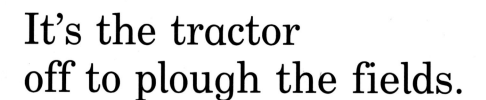

Sam can hear a running noise.
What can that be?

It's the rabbit
running home.

Where are her babies?

Sam can hear a moo-ing noise.
What can that be?

It's the cow
in the barn.

Where is her calf?

Sam can hear an oinking noise.
What can that be?

It's the pig
in the pigsty.

Where are her piglets?

Sam can hear a clucking noise.
What can that be?

It's the hen
in the henhouse.

Where are her chicks?

Sam can hear a baa-ing noise.
What can that be?

It's the sheep
in the field.

Where is her lamb?

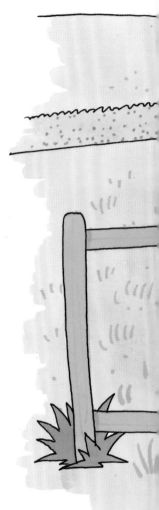

Sam can hear a quacking noise.
What can that be?

It's the duck
by the pond.

Where are her ducklings?

The sun is up now, and it's getting hot.
Everything is quiet on the farm.

But listen...
There's a loud snoring noise
coming from the barn!

Who can that be?

Shh! Let's leave him to sleep!